It's Your Turn, Roger!

Susanna Gretz

THE BODLEY HEAD

London

In all the flats in Roger's house
it's nearly supper time.

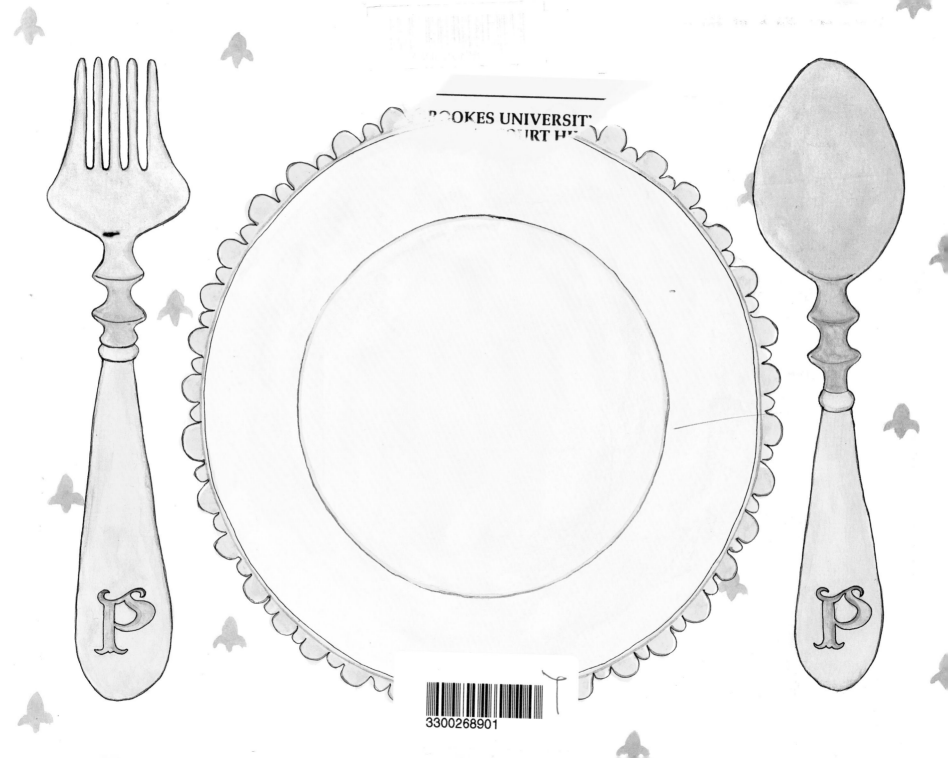

ALSO BY SUSANNA GRETZ

Roger Takes Charge!
Roger Loses His Marbles!
Roger Mucks In!

British Library Cataloguing
in Publication Data
Gretz, Susanna
It's your turn, Roger!
I. Title
823'.914[J]   PZ7
ISBN 0–370–30621–X

Roger, it's your turn
to set the table.

That's his sister calling.

I see you, Roger!

That's his little brother.

Roger, you know we
all take turns at helping.

That's Roger's dad.

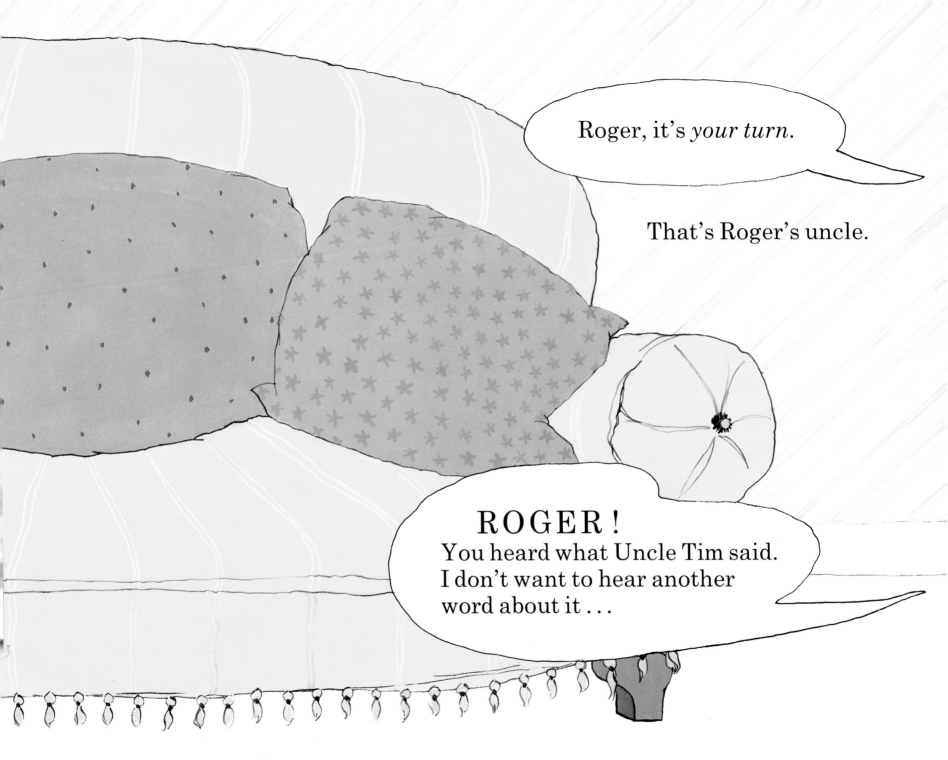

"OK, OK," moans Roger.

"In other families you don't have to help," Roger grumbles.
"Are you sure?" asks Uncle Tim. "Why don't you go and see?"

"All right, I *will*," says Roger.

He stomps out of the door . . .

... and on upstairs.

"Come in, come in," says the family on the first floor.

"Do I have to set the table?" asks Roger.

"Certainly not, you're a guest. Come in and have some fishmeal soup."

What a fancy supper table, thinks Roger ...

. . . but what *horrible* soup!
"Excuse me," says Roger, and he hops upstairs.

"Come in, come in," says the family on the second floor.

"Do I have to set the table?" asks Roger.

"Certainly not, you're a guest. Come in and have some mud pancakes."

What a messy table, thinks Roger ...
and what *dreadful* pancakes!

No one notices as he slips out.

"Come in, come in," says
the family on the third floor.
"Do I have to set the table?"
asks Roger.
"Certainly not, you're a guest.
Come in and have a little snack."

This family doesn't even *have* a table . . .

Roots and snails – YUK!
Roger hurries away.

"Come in, come in,"says
the family in the top flat.
    "Do I have to set the table?"
asks Roger.
    "Certainly not, you're a guest.
Come in and have some milky mush."
    "Well . . ." says Roger.
He *is* getting hungry.

Everyone in the top flat is busy
getting the supper table ready.

Roger sits by himself
and watches.
    If I weren't a "guest",
I could help too, he thinks.

"What's a guest?" he asks someone.
"Well . . . guests don't really live here."
"Oh," says Roger. "Now where *I* live . . ."

Just then a special smell creeps all
the way upstairs to the top flat.

"Where *I* live," shouts Roger, "there's
something *good* for supper –"

"—and it's my turn to help!"

"I took your turn for you," says
Uncle Tim.
"I'll take your turn tomorrow,"
says Roger, between mouthfuls.

Worm pie for dessert – whoopee! Roger's favourite.